MONSTER TALES OF NATIVE AMERICANS

Library of Congress Catalog Card Number: 78-5234

International Standard Book Numbers:
   0-913940-85-2 Library Bound
   0-89686-006-X Paperback

Edited by - Dr. Howard Schroeder
         Prof. in Reading and Language Arts
         Dept. of Elementary Education
         Mankato State University

Layout and Design - Barb Furan

MONSTER TALES OF NATIVE AMERICANS

CIP

Library of Congress
Cataloging in Publication Data

Thorne, Ian.
   Monster Tales Of Native Americans.

   (Search for the Unknown)
   SUMMARY: A collection of monster stories from various
North American Indian tribes.
   1. Indians of North America--Legends. 2. Animals,
Mythical--Juvenile literature. 3. Monsters--Juvenile
literature. (1. Indians of North America--Legends. 2.
Monsters--Fiction. 3. Animals, Mythical--Fiction) I. Furan,
Barbara Howell. II. Title. III. Series.
E98.F6T43   398.2'45   78-5234
ISBN 0-913940-85-2

MONSTER TALES OF NATIVE AMERICANS

by Ian Thorne

Illustrations by
Barbara Howell Furan

LEGENDS OF MONSTERS

Modern people like to go to horror movies and read ghost stories. It is fun to be scared, just a little.

The Native Americans of long ago had their monster tales, too. During the winter, when storms kept the people inside their lodges, story-telling helped pass the time.

Some monster stories explained events of nature such as volcanoes or waterfalls. Still other monster legends were used to show why a certain thing was true. For example, why the mosquitoes in New York and New Jersey are so fierce.

The best monster tales were passed on from grandparents to grandchildren, from village to village, even from tribe to tribe. It was common for many Indian nations to have similar stories.

By the twentieth century, several Native Americans were giving up their old ways of living. They were no longer telling the old tales. So that the legends would not be lost, scientists went to the oldest of their people and had them repeat the tales. The stories were gathered and made into books for the first time.

In this book are monster stories from several different tribes. At the end of each story, you will find a paragraph or two about the people who used to tell the tale.

THE SPIRIT LAKE DEMONS

It had been a bad summer for the Yakima people. No rain had fallen. The rivers were so low there were few fish to be caught. The berry bushes were dry, with very little fruit. Game animals were scarce in the valleys where the villages were.

One day in early autumn, the people in one village were nearly starving. The strong young men said they would go out to look for meat. They would go far to the west, toward the cone-shaped mountain named Loo-wit.

One young hunter saw the tracks of a huge elk. His heart filled with hope. He followed the animal for many miles to the very base of Loo-wit. Once, he caught a glimpse of the elk. It was larger than any he had seen before. If he could kill it, there would be meat for the whole village.

Around the hunter, the forest was very still. Suddenly, the young man smelled a strange smell. He became afraid because the smell belonged to the terrible Sayatkah!

The Yakima people and their neighbors, the Klickitat, told stories of the demon Sayatkah. These were tall, very hairy, and known for their bad smell. The Sayatkah would come at night to steal salmon from Indian drying racks. They left giant footprints. If you let them alone, they would not harm you. But if the Indians killed a Sayatkah, the other demons would come during the night and roll big stones onto the In-

dian lodges. Twelve Indians would die for each slain
Sayatkah.

The young hunter was full of fear. Even so, he
followed the trail of the elk. At last he came to the lake
that lay at the foot of Loo-wit. It was late evening. The
footprints of the elk went to the very edge of the
water.

"What shall I do?" the young hunter wondered.

A moment later, he saw something. It was the elk, swimming in the misty waters not far from shore. It was the largest elk the young Indian had ever seen.

He took his bow and let an arrow fly. The elk was hit! It leaped in the water, then quietly floated. The young hunter knew it would sink within a moment and be lost. There was only one thing to do.

The smell of the Sayatkah was strong in the evening air, but the young man threw down his weapons and dived into the lake. He had a rawhide rope in his teeth which he would tie around the antlers of the elk.

The young man swam toward the elk, but it seemed to float farther and farther away, into the mist. He, growing weary, followed it nearly to the middle of the lake. The bottomless waters were very cold. Above the swimmer loomed the slopes of the mountain streaked with snow in the moonlight.

"I can swim no farther," the tired hunter thought. "I must return to the shore."

Suddenly, he heard a horrid sound of laughter. At the edge of the lake, huge hairy forms were jumping up and down and laughing. Mist rose up all around the young man and he felt something grab his ankles under the water.

He cried out. But slowly, slowly, something pulled him down. As he disappeared, the form of the elk turned to mist and faded away like a ghost.

And the Sayatkah laughed . . .

On certain nights each year, it is said that the phantoms of the elk and the drowned hunter can still be seen, hovering in the mists above Spirit Lake. The Sayatkah still live among the snows of Loo-wit, too. But nowadays, they are called Bigfoot because of their huge footprints.

The mountain called Loo-wit is now known as Mount St. Helens. Spirit Lake, at its northern base, was regarded with dread by all of the Indian tribes of that part of the state of Washington. The Yakima lived west of the big bend in the Columbia River. They and their southern neighbors, the Klickitat, had a hunting-fishing culture. They had horses and lived in lodges made of wood. Bigfoot is still said to wander the remote areas of the Cascade Range in Washington and Oregon.

THE RIVER MONSTER

Two young men of the Cheyenne went off to explore, as young men will. They traveled so far that they lost their way. At the end of day, they came to a grassland where they made camp.

One young man made a fire while the other searched for something to eat. Finally, he discovered two very large eggs hidden in the grass.

"See what I have found," he said to his friend. "Each one is big enough for a whole meal!"

"I don't like the looks of them," the other boy said. I don't think we ought to eat those eggs."

But the first boy only laughed. He roasted the eggs in the fire and cracked one open. "They are very good," he said taking a mouthful. "Have some."

But the second boy would not share the egg. His friend ate one whole egg and most of the second one. Then the two boys went to sleep.

In the morning, the young man who had eaten the eggs said: "I feel stiff and sore. My legs hurt."

His friend drew off his moccasins and leggings. The boy who had eaten the eggs had strange skin on his feet and lower legs. It was brown and scaly.

"We must go home," said the sick boy.

The two of them set out at once. However, the boy with the sore legs walked slower and slower. Finally, he had to crawl along.

"I think I would feel better if my legs were wet," he said, so the two made camp by a little lake.

The sick boy crept down to the water. He soon began to feel much better. He swam and dived until the sun went down and his friend called:

"Come out now, or you will get tired."

As the sick boy came to shore, his friend gave a cry of horror. The sick boy's legs had grown together.

From the waist down, he looked like a huge, scaly snake.

The snake-boy was frightened. "Don't leave me," he said to his friend. "If you do, I will surely die."

"I will not leave you," his friend said.

The next morning, the two boys resumed their journey together home. Whenever they came to a lake or river, the snake-boy would rest in the water. More and more of his body became that of a snake.

"There is somewhere I must go!" the snake-boy gasped. "I am being called. You must help me get to the place where I must go."

His friend agreed to help him. For several more days, the snake-boy crawled along. His friend helped him. And at last they came to the Mississippi River.

"This is the place," the snake-boy said. "Let us rest for the night."

When the sun came up, the snake-boy was gone. His friend stood on the bank of the wide river and called the snake-boy by name.

And from the water arose a head. It was covered

with blue scales. There were two horns above black glittering eyes, and a forked tongue that flickered in and out.

"Do not be afraid," said the snake. "It is I. The spirits have told me that I must be the guardian of this river. You must return to our people and tell them."

"I will," said his friend.

The snake said, "Whenever the people cross water, tell them to drop in a bit of food or tobacco as a gift for me. If they do that, I will bless them."

Then the two friends said their last good-bye, and the huge snake sank down into the deep water. And ever after, the Cheyenne people dropped gifts into the water for the snake-man whenever they crossed large rivers.

Ancient traditions place the homeland of the Cheyenne in Minnesota. Later, they were forced westward into the prairie of South Dakota. This story must date from these very early days. When the white man encountered the Cheyenne, they were the great buffalo hunters of the northern Great Plains, ranging from Nebraska into Colorado and Wyoming.

THE GIANT MOSQUITO

The Tuscarora Indians of old New York suffered from a monster mosquito. The insect was so huge it could carry away full-grown men. Night after night it raided the villages, flying away with people and sucking them dry of blood.

The Indians prayed: "O Holder of the Heavens, come and drive away this Grandfather Mosquito!"

The Holder of the Heavens heard their prayer. He came down and did battle with the mosquito. They fought hard, stamping their feet into the solid rock and making footprints. Finally, near Lake Onondaga, the Sky Holder killed the giant insect.

Its blood poured onto the sands around the lake. And from the blood came millions and millions of smaller mosquitoes. They stung Holder of the Heavens and he fled back to the Sky Country to get away from them.

But the people on earth could not escape from the mosquitoes. Ever since then, the mosquitoes in New York and New Jersey have been the largest and most fierce in the whole world!

The mosquitoes of this region are still legendary. Footprints in solid rock, made by dinosaurs a long time ago, were said by the Indians to belong to Holder of the Sky and Grandfather Mosquito.

Many years ago, the Tuscarora lived in New York. They migrated to North Carolina, where the early settlers battled with them. The defeated tribe moved back to New York in the early 1700's, joining the Iroquois Confederation.

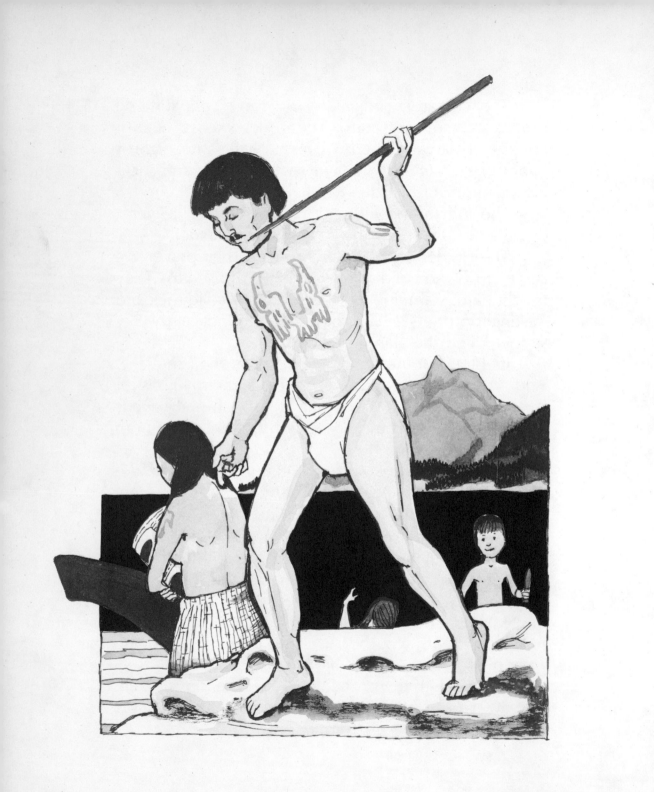

DEVILFISH'S DAUGHTER

A young Haida warrior named Gitlin went fishing with his wife and two small children. They needed bait for their hooks. So they landed their boat on a small rocky island.

Gitlin and his wife speared small devilfish, a kind of octopus, and put them into a basket. Once they were cut up, the devilfish made good bait.

"You take the children now and go to the boat," Gitlin said. "I want to see what is on the other side of this cliff."

He went climbing over the slippery rocks. The tide was low. Seaweed, starfish, and mussels lay on the beach. There he found a cave! Gitlin decided to go inside. Sometimes the waves cast wonderful things into caves, things from faraway lands.

He climbed carefully over the rocks. There were green shadows on the roof of the cave. Waves made strange sucking sounds. Gitlin thought he saw something shining in the back of the cave. He waded into water above his knees. Toward the back of the cave, the water became deeper and deeper.

Then, in the green gloom, he felt something touch him. A long, long arm reached out of an opening in the rocks. It wound around his leg. Another tentacle wrapped itself around his body.

Gitlin felt himself being pulled into the black waters, deep inside the cave.

Gitlin's wife waited in vain for him to come back. The tide turned. She walked along the shore trying to find him, but the cave was gone. The rising waters of the tide had covered it.

Weeping, she put the children into the boat. She went back to the village to tell the other Haida what had happened.

Meanwhile, Gitlin was having a strange adventure.

He woke up at the bottom of the sea. Beside him sat a strange maiden with long, black hair. She smiled at him. Her fingers touched his face. Gitlin shuddered when he saw that the fingers had no bones.

"Who are you?" Gitlin asked.

"I am Hanax, daughter of the Devilfish Demon," she said.

"Let me go!" said the frightened man.

But Hanax said, "I have waited long for a mate, and now my father has brought you to me. Come, he is waiting for us."

She took Gitlin and pulled him through the green waters. They came to a cave surrounded with seaweed. There, on a cushion of seaweed, sat a huge black octopus. His eyes glittered brightly.

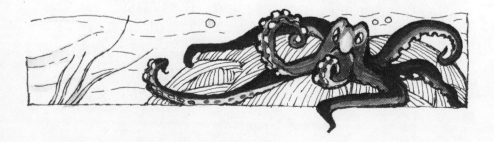

"You will marry my child," said the Devilfish Demon to Gitlin. "You are a lucky man, for she is Princess of the Sea."

"Great Chief," Gitlin said, "this world of yours terrifies me. I am not used to it. Let me go back to my own world of sunshine and air."

At first, the Devilfish refused. However, Gitlin was so unhappy that the Devilfish's daughter took pity on him.

"Let him go back to his home for awhile," she begged. "Then he will return to me."

Finally, the Devilfish agreed. He said: "Do not forget your promise to return. If you do forget, a dreadful thing will happen to you."

Gitlin promised. The Devilfish's daughter brought two canoes. She sat in one, Gitlin in the other. The boats moved swiftly without anyone paddling. In a

short time, Hanax and Gitlin came to the shore near the Haida village.

She waved good-bye to him with her boneless fingers. Gitlin could only think of his wife and children. He ran into the village shouting their names.

The people were filled with joy. They welcomed Gitlin back. The next day, when Gitlin returned to the canoe, he found it was filled with beautiful gifts from Hanax.

Days went by, then weeks. Gitlin was a rich man. The villagers thought much of him. His wife and children were very happy. Sometimes Gitlin would remember the Devilfish's daughter. But then he would think: "Surely I do not have to return to her yet. I will stay here awhile longer."

One night there was a great feast. The Haida people were inside their great wooden house, singing. Then the door opened —

Gitlin screamed. A black shadow came in and flowed up to him.

The people watched in horror as Gitlin began to change. His arms and legs became boneless. They grew longer, and darker. Four tentacles sprouted from his body. His head shrank down and became one with his body. Of his face, only two huge eyes, filled with fear remained.

The octopus slithered frantically for the door. The people got out of its way. But when they looked toward the shore, they saw two figures, one a huge octopus, the other a slender maiden.

The figure of the maiden changed. All at once, there were two devilfish on the shore. They got into two canoes that waited on the beach. Then the boats raced away, without anyone paddling, and were never seen again.

The Haida Indians lived on the Queen Charlotte Islands off the western coast of British Columbia. They were among the most famous of the totem-pole tribes. The Haida made a comfortable living by using the riches of the sea.

THE OWL MONSTER

Once there were two naughty children named White Swan and Otter. They lived among the Shahaptin people a long time ago.

The children's mother said: "White Swan, fetch water from the river." But White Swan only laughed. Then she ran away and hid.

The mother said: "Otter, since your sister is so wicked, you will have to fetch the water."

But the little boy said: "I won't! That's girls' work!" He too, ran away and hid.

The mother was very tired and angry. Since she had magic powers, she decided to teach her bad children a lesson. As they watched from hiding places among the bushes, they saw their mother change into a raven!

"I will fly away from you, naughty children!" the mother said. "You will be sorry you did not obey."

And the raven flapped its wings and flew off into the sky.

White Swan and Otter were frightened. They came out of their hiding places. Quickly, White Swan went for the water while Otter gathered firewood. Their mother still did not come back.

The sun began to go down. By this time the children's father had returned from hunting. "Where is your mother?" he asked.

The children began to cry. "She has changed into a raven and flown away," wailed Otter.

"It is all our fault," said White Swan. "We were bad and would not obey her."

At that the father became very angry. "I will have to go after your mother and find her," he said. He changed into a raven and flew out of the smoke-hole of the tepee. The children were left all alone.

The next morning, the children decided they would have to go to Dawn Man, their uncle, and ask him to help them. Dawn Man was a powerful shaman, with magic powers. He would know how to call their mother and father home again.

The two children set out through the thick forest. It was a fearful journey.

They heard a deep hooting sound, and there was a mysterious rushing of wings.

"The Owl Monster lives in these woods," said Otter. "If we don't hurry, he will catch us!"

The children came to the bank of a wide river. On the other side was the tepee of Dawn Man. His canoe lay drawn up before it on the bank.

"Uncle! Uncle!" called Otter. "Come and get us!" The shaman came out of his tepee. He saw the children. But he saw something else, too.

"Run, children, run!" called Dawn Man. "The Owl Monster is coming after you!"

White Swan and Otter looked up. They saw a great white owl, larger than a man, swooping down at them. Its eyes flashed and it made terrible hoots and howls. Its cruel claws reached out to tear the children apart.

Dawn Man jumped into his canoe. He crossed the river. Then he grabbed his medicine club and began to fight with the Owl Monster.

But his magic was not strong enough. The children wept bitterly as the Owl Monster slashed at their poor, brave uncle.

Suddenly two calls rang out: "Craaa! Craaa!" Two ravens came out of the sky and began to peck at the Owl Monster's eyes. When it could not see, the ravens forced the Owl Monster into the river. With its wings heavy and wet, the Owl Monster sank beneath the waters, never to return.

Dawn Man was badly hurt. The children gave him his medicine bundle. The shaman touched his magic stick. All at once, his wounds were healed. Then Dawn Man used the magic stick to touch the ravens.

"Mother! Father! cried the children. The ravens were gone, and in their place stood the children's parents.

Otter and White Swan ran into their parents' arms. "We will never be naughty again," they promised.

And the mother and father said, "We will never go away again."

Dawn Man invited them all to his tepee for a feast. After that, the two children always obeyed their mother and father.

This Indian story is very similar to stories told by the people of Europe. Perhaps it shows that naughty children are found among all human races.

The Shahaptin Indian language was spoken by the tribes of the northern Rocky Mountains and the Northern Plateau. Nations such as the Nez Perce, Palouse, Cayuse, and Walla Walla hunted buffalo, elk, and other animals, as well as catching fish in the mountain rivers.

THE HORNED LIZARD

A band of Moqui or Hopi Indians lived in the southwestern desert. They had their village high on top of a mesa, or tableland. All around the mesa were deep canyons which were believed to be full of monsters.

The Moquis made gardens on top of the mesa, and watered the corn and squash from a flowing spring. Their village was pleasant and green. But the canyons below were dry, and provided no food.

The monsters decided to climb up to the top of the mesa and steal food from the Moquis. They came very quietly in the middle of the night. They stole corn — and they stole people, too. The next morning, the monsters were gone, but they left corn cobs and human bones behind them!

The chief of the Moquis said: "The man who kills these monsters shall have great riches. And he will be given the most beautiful maiden for his wife."

Many brave warriors set out to fight with the man-eating monsters. But none of the warriors came back alive.

Finally a young man named Lolomi said he would go. Some of the Moqui fighting men laughed at this, for Lolomi was known for his kind heart.

"The monsters will eat you up, bones and all!" they said. Lolomi said he would go anyway.

The young man traveled down the steep trail that led from the top of the mesa. After awhile he heard a sad squeaking noise. There was a horned lizard lying

beside the trail. A rock had fallen on the lizard and pinned it to the ground.

"Go free, little brother," said Lolomi. He lifted the rock off the lizard and started to walk on.

But suddenly there was a voice, which said: "Lolomi! Would you like to destroy the monsters?"

"I would," Lolomi said, looking around to see who was talking with him. He saw no one.

"Take my horned crest for a helmet!" said the voice. Lolomi discovered that the loud voice was coming from the little horned lizard.

The young man reached out and took the lizard's crest. It swelled up and became large, like a thick leather helmet studded with sharp horns. Lolomi put it on.

"Now take my back armor!" said the horned lizard.

Lolomi reached out his hand. The knobby armor of the little animal came away and became large enough to wear. The lizard sat there in a smooth skin. Lolomi put on its body armor.

"Now go and fight the monsters," said the lizard.

Lolomi did as he was told. He came upon one of the man-eaters, gnawing on a bone. When the monster saw Lolomi in his horny armor, he gave a squawk of fear. Lolomi came after him. The monster tossed a spear at Lolomi, however, it only bounced from his armor.

The monster decided Lolomi must be a Lizard Spirit. He ran away, making a loud, sharp noise, and fell over the edge of a cliff.

Lolomi went after the rest of the monsters. They tried to kill Lolomi with knives and clubs, but the horned-lizard armor was too strong. He crowded the

monsters close to the edge of the steep canyon walls. One by one, they fell to their deaths.

On the mesa above, the Moqui people heard the yells of the monsters. They came down. All they found was Lolomi and a pile of dead monsters! They did not notice a little horned lizard sitting beside Lolomi on a rock.

"We will make Lolomi our chief!" cried the people.

"I will be Lolomi's wife," said the fairest maiden.

And they all returned happily to the top of the mesa. But the little horned lizard only scampered away.

The Moqui or Hopi people still live on the mesas in northern Arizona. Their villages, called pueblos, are composed of large stone or adobe buildings that look like apartment houses. The people have long been known for their beautiful pottery and weaving. They were wealthy farmers, and their wealth often attracted raiding parties from other tribes.

THE LITTLE PEOPLE

A little Micmac girl came running up to her wig-wam in the eastern forest.

"Mother! Look what I have found!"

She held out a tiny canoe. Sitting inside it was a tiny man with a tiny paddle!

"Take him back at once!" said the mother. "It is one of the Little People! He will do us harm!"

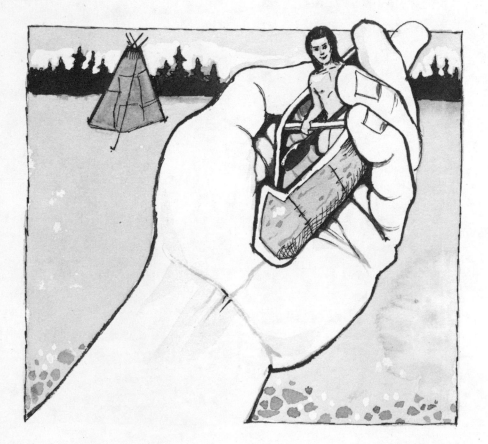

The girl did as she was told. Gently, she set the tiny canoe into the river. The tiny man gave her a cheerful wave. "I'll come back and play with you," he promised. Then he paddled swiftly away.

The girl told her mother what the tiny man had said, but the mother replied: "Never have anything to do with the Little People. They have magic that we do not understand."

The little girl promised, but the next time that she went to the river, she saw the tiny canoe again. This time, the tiny man had an even tinier child with him. Both of the Little People were friendly. They played with the girl for a long time.

"I don't see why my mother is afraid of you," the girl said. "You are good and kind."

After that, the girl saw the Little People often. One day when she went to the river, she saw a whole fleet of tiny canoes. Little men, women and children were riding in them.

"Would you like to see our village?" asked one of the Little People. "It is just across the river."

"Oh, yes!" said the happy girl.

"Step into our canoe," said a little man.

"But I am too big," the girl said.

"No you aren't," replied the little man. "Come."

The girl stepped carefully. As soon as she touched the canoe, it seemed to grow as large as any other Micmac canoe. She went happily off with her new friends.

That evening, the girl's mother came to look for her. She called and called, but her daughter did not answer.

The mother's heart was full of fear as she saw footprints in the sand on the river bank. They were the prints of a little girl. But as they came close to the water, they shrank. Smaller and smaller the footprints became, until they were no longer than a thumbnail. There at the water's edge the tiny prints vanished.

And the little girl was never seen again.

The Micmacs were a northeastern woodland people living in what are now the Canadian provinces of New Brunswick, Nova Scotia, Quebec, and eastern Ontario. They hunted deer and other animals, and gathered wild plants for food. The Micmacs were the first Native Americans met by early Canadian settlers.

THE FROGS OF FORBIDDEN MOUNTAIN

Two young boys of the Mohave tribe went off hunting mountain sheep. One was named Shy Owl, the other Fast Lance.

They walked over the dry hills above the desert, but found no game. At last they came to the base of Forbidden Mountain.

"Monsters are supposed to live in there," Shy Owl said. "But there are no sheep out here. Shall we look for them on the mountain?"

Fast Lance said, "Yes." The two boys began to climb. Before night fell, they had shot two fine sheep. They made camp. For fear of the monsters, they decided to take turns sleeping. Fast Lance had the first watch.

As the fire burned low, Fast Lance's eyes began to close. Soon he was fast asleep. His snores mingled with those of Shy Owl . . .

Then both boys woke up in terror.

Their arms were tied. They were helpless. And there in front of them were two creatures. They were about the size of buck deer, but were shaped like huge frogs!

"You must come with us," said one of the frogs. It spoke the Mohave tongue, but with a croaking accent.

The two boys stumbled along a rocky path that led deep into the Forbidden Mountain. After a long time, they came to a dark lake. The frogs tied the boys to logs.

"Our village is on the other side of the lake," croaked the leader-frog. "Come!"

Towed by the swimming frogs, the boys crossed the water. On the other side they were met by a crowd of frog-people. Houses, built of mud, lined the lake shore.

The captives were led to a cave in the hillside. A strong door was opened and the boys were pushed inside. At first they could not see, but heard men's voices speaking different languages.

"Who's there?" said Shy Owl.

"We are Navaho and Zuni and Pima," said a voice.

"We are Hopi and Apachi and Paiute. We are all prisoners of the frog monsters."

The boys were untied as they listened to the amazing stories of the other prisoners.

"The frog monsters keep us as we keep horses," said a Navaho man. "They use us as racing animals. If we do not run swiftly, we are killed. The frogs have kidnapped travellers from all parts of the Forbidden Mountain Range."

In the morning, Fast Lance and Shy Owl found out this was true. Each boy had a small saddle placed on his back. Then frog-children climbed upon them and guided their human mounts to a lakeside race track for practice.

The boys learned something as they trotted along. The lake had a log dam at one end. The sight of the dam gave Fast Lance an idea.

"If one of us swims down and pulls out the key log," he thought, "the rest of the dam will come apart.

We could each grab a log, and the flood waters would carry us quickly out of this place."

After a time, the frogs had a big day of racing. All of the human steeds ran swiftly and the frog people cheered and made bets. When the races were over, the frogs began to feast and drink.

"This is our chance," said Shy Owl. The two boys told the other prisoners to get ready. Then they set out to destroy the dam.

The prisoners crouched at the edge of the frog race track. The monsters paid no attention to them. They did not see the two boys swim out into the lake.

Suddenly there was a great roaring sound. Log after log shot into the air as the dam broke apart. All of the men ran for the water. They clung to the logs that swept by. The roaring waters rushed through a cleft in the mountain wall and spilled into the valley far below. The frog monsters stood with open mouths. Their lake

drained away, leaving them high and dry on the shore. The prisoners had escaped with the water.

The water spread out on the valley floor and the men let go of the logs. They reached dry land. Then they all set out on different paths, back to their homelands.

Shy Owl and Fast Lance went back to their village. The Mohave people were surprised when the boys told their story. A big party of armed warriors went into the Forbidden Mountains to find the frog monsters and kill them.

But when they reached the spot, they found that all the frogs were gone. All that was left was the empty race track, which some people say is still there today.

The Mojave tribe lived along the lower Colorado River in what is now western Arizona and southeastern California. A warlike people, they were also great traders with those living east and west of their lands. They grew corn and beans and also hunted for a living.

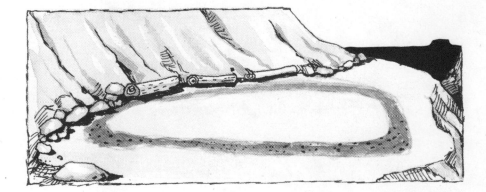

THUNDERER AND THE FEVER-MONSTER

Long ago, the Seneca people lived along the banks of the Niagara River. They were very happy until a fever began to strike them. The shaman's medicine was powerless to drive the fever away, and many of the Seneca people died.

In one Seneca village lived a beautiful maiden. Her father said she must marry an old, ugly man. But the girl said, "I would rather give myself to the river!"

She jumped into a canoe and pushed off without a paddle. The churning waters of the Niagara carried her toward the rapids, where she would surely be killed.

Thunderer, the spirit of clouds and rain, lived in a cave beneath the rapids. When he saw the girl floating toward death, he took pity on her. He spread his mighty wings and took her out of the canoe. A moment later, the boat disappeared beneath the white water.

Thunderer took the girl to his cave where he treated her with kindness. "The old man will die soon," said Thunderer. "Then you may return safely to your people."

"I may escape from one danger," said the girl, "but there is still the fever."

"I will tell you why there is sickness in your village," said the Thunderer. "A fever-monster lives in the earth beneath it. He poisons the water."

Thunderer told the girl that the fever-monster was shaped like a huge snake. No human could hope to kill it.

"Then you must help us," the girl begged. "Please do not let all my people die."

Thunderer said he would think about that. He told the girl she might go home safely. She left the cave and told the Seneca people all that Thunderer had said. The people prayed that Thunderer would come and kill the fever-monster.

That night there was a big storm. Lightning flashed as bright as day and thunder made the people cover their ears in fear. Again and again the lightning-bolts hit the ground of the Seneca village.

In the morning, the storm was over. The Seneca people came out of their lodges to see what had happened.

There on the ground was a huge serpent, stone dead. It was twenty arrow-flights long.

"The fever-monster has been slain by Thunderer!" cried the people happily. "Come, let us get rid of its body. We will put it into the river."

The whole village worked very hard to drag the huge snake to the Niagara. They pushed the body into the water. It began to float downstream.

When it came to the rapids, the snake's body got stuck. It became wedged between two points of rock. The river rose up, then poured over the snake which formed a great waterfall.

"Listen to the sound of the waterfall!" said the maiden. "It speaks in the voice of the one who saved us!"

Ever afterward, the Seneca people were free of the fever. And ever afterward, mighty Niagara Falls spoke with the voice of the Thunderer.

The Seneca were the westernmost tribe of New York's famous Iroquois Confederation. The people were clever hunters who lived in wigwams covered with bark. The fever told of in this legend may have been brought in by early white explorers or traders.

INVESTIGATE THE OTHER FINE BOOKS IN THIS SERIES

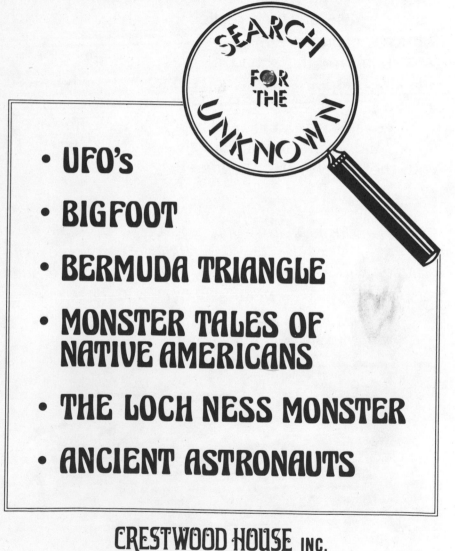

- UFO's
- BIGFOOT
- BERMUDA TRIANGLE
- MONSTER TALES OF NATIVE AMERICANS
- THE LOCH NESS MONSTER
- ANCIENT ASTRONAUTS

CRESTWOOD HOUSE INC.

P.O. BOX 3427   MANKATO, MN 56001